MR. PUNCH IN THE HUNTING FIELD

AS PICTURED BY

JOHN LEECH, CHARLES KEENE, PHIL MAY, RANDOLPH CALDECOTT, L. RAVEN-HILL, G. D. ARMOUR, G. H. JALLAND, ARTHUR HOPKINS, REGINALD CLEAVER, CECIL ALDIN, TOM BROWNE, W. L. HODGSON AND OTHERS

WITH 173 ILLUSTRATIONS

PUBLISHED BY ARRANGEMENT WITH

THE PROPRIETORS OF "PUNCH"

THE EDUCATIONAL BOOK CO. LTD.

PUNCH LIBRARY OF HUMOUR

*Twenty-five volumes, crown 8vo, 192 pages
fully Illustrated*

LIFE IN LONDON
COUNTRY LIFE
IN THE HIGHLANDS
SCOTTISH HUMOUR
IRISH HUMOUR
COCKNEY HUMOUR
IN SOCIETY
AFTER DINNER STORIES
IN BOHEMIA
AT THE PLAY
MR. PUNCH AT HOME
ON THE CONTINONG
RAILWAY BOOK
AT THE SEASIDE
MR. PUNCH AFLOAT
IN THE HUNTING FIELD
MR. PUNCH ON TOUR
WITH ROD AND GUN
MR. PUNCH AWHEEL
BOOK OF SPORTS
GOLF STORIES
IN WIG AND GOWN
ON THE WARPATH
BOOK OF LOVE
WITH THE CHILDREN

EDITOR'S NOTE

FROM his earliest days MR. PUNCH has been an enthusiast for the Hunting Field. But in this he has only been the faithful recorder of the manners of his countrymen, as there is no sport more redolent of "Merrie England" than that of the Horse and Hound. At no time in MR. PUNCH's history has he been without an artist who has specialised in the humours of the hunt. First it was the inimitable Leech, some of whose drawings find a place in the present collection, and then the mantle of the sporting artist would seem to have descended to feminine shoulders, as Miss Bowers (Mrs. Bowers-Edwards) wore it for some ten years after 1866. That lady is also represented in the present work, at pages 49 and 111. Later came Mr. G. H. Jalland, many of whose drawings we have chosen for inclusion here. Perhaps the most popular of his hunting jokes was that of the Frenchman exclaiming, "Stop ze chasse! I tomble, I faloff! *Stop ze fox!!!*" (see page 141). To-day, of course, it is Mr. G. D. Armour whose pencil is devoted chiefly to illustrating the humorous side of hunting; but now, as formerly, most of the eminent artists whose work lies usually in other fields, delight at times to find a subject associated with the hunt. Thus we are able to present examples of Mr. Cecil Aldin and Mr. Raven-Hill in sportive mood, while such celebrities of the past as Randolph Caldecott and Phil May are here drawn upon for the enriching of this, the first book of hunting humour compiled from the abundant chronicles of MR. PUNCH.

5

'ARRY OUT WITH THE 'OUNDS

MR. PUNCH IN THE HUNTING FIELD

THE HUNTING SEASON

(By Jorrocks Junior)

THE season for hunting I see has begun,
So adieu for a time to my rod and my gun;
And ho! for the fox, be he wild or in bag,
As I follow the chase on my high-mettled nag.

"WEATHER PERMITTING,"—MR. PUNCH DRIVES TO THE
FIRST MEET.

7

Mr. Punch in the Hunting Field

I call him high-mettled, but still I must state,
He hasn't a habit I always did hate,
He doesn't walk sideways, like some "gees" you meet,
Who go slantindicularly down the street.

He's steady and well broken in, for, of course,
I can't risk my life on an unbroken horse;
You might tie a torpedo or two on behind,
And though they exploded that horse wouldn't mind

My strong point is costume, and oft I confess
I've admired my get-up in a sportsmanlike dress;
Though, but for the finish their lustre confers,
I would much rather be, I declare, without spurs.

They look very well as to cover you ride,
But I can't keep the things from the animal's side;
And the mildest of "gees," I am telling no fibs,
Will resent having liberties ta'en with his ribs.

Then hie to the cover, the dogs are all there,
And the horn of the hunter is heard on the air;
I've a horn of my own, which in secret I stow,
For, oddly enough, they don't like me to blow.

We'll go round by that gate, my good sir, if you please,
I'm one of your sportsmen who rides at his ease;
And I don't care to trouble my courser to jump,
For whenever he does I fall off in a lump.

Then haste to the meet ! The Old Berkeley shall find,
If I don't go precisely as fast as the wind,
If they 'll give my Bucephalus time to take breath,
We shall both of us, sometimes, be in at the death !

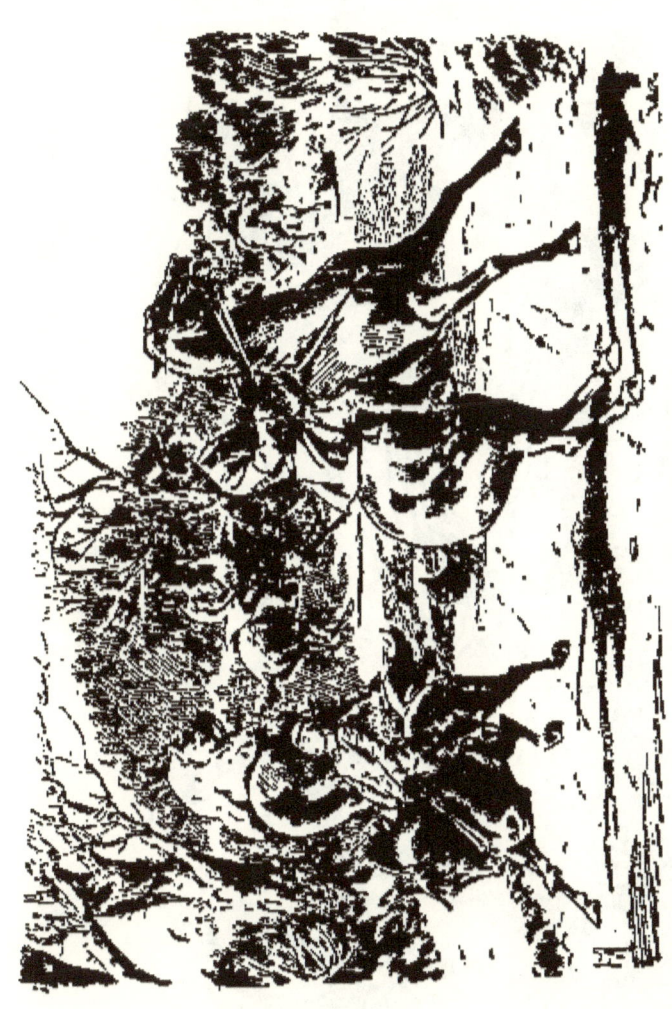

A LION IN THE PATH?

Oh dear no! Merely the "*first open day*" after a long frost, and a tom-tit has been inconsiderate enough to fly suddenly out of the fence on the way to covert!

TRIALS OF A NOVICE

Unsympathetic Bystander. "Taking 'Im back to 'is cab, guv'nor?"

HOW THE LAST RUN OF THE WOPSHIRE HOUNDS WAS SPOILT.

PROVERBS FOR THE TIMID HUNTSMAN

Dressing

THERE'S no toe without a corn.
If the boot pinches—bear it.

Breakfast

A snack in time, saves nine.
Faint hunger never conquered tough beef-steak.

Mounting

You can't make a hunter out of a hired hack.
The nearer the ground the safer the seat.

In the Field

Take care of the hounds, but the fence may take care of itself.
Too many brooks spoil the sport.
One pair of spurs may bring a horse to the water, but twenty will not make him jump.
It is the howl that shows the funk.
Fools break rails for wise men to go over.
Snobs and their saddles are soon parted.

REALLY PLEASANT!

Six miles from home, horse dead lame, awfully tender
feet, and horribly tight boots.

"Now, if I jump it, I shall certainly fall off; and if I dismount to open it, I shall never get on again."

At Luncheon

A flask in the hand is worth a cask in the vault.
Cut your sandwiches according to your stomach.

Coming Home

The nearer the home, the harder the seat.

Bed-time

It's a heavy sleep that has no turning.

This is Jones, who thought to slip down by the rail
early in the morning, and have a gallop with the fox
hounds. On looking out of window, he finds it is a clear
frosty morning. He sees a small boy sliding—actually
sliding on the pavement opposite!! and—doesn't he hate
that boy—and doesn't he say it is a beastly climate!!

NEW SPORTING DICTIONARY OF FAMILIAR LATIN PHRASES.

(1) Labour omnia vincit. (Labor overcomes everything.)

(2) Ars est celare artem. "Aprés vous, mademoiselle!"

(3)   Exeunt Omnes.   (They all go off.)

A Genuine Sportswoman

Mrs. Shodditon (to Captain Forrard, on a cub-hunting morning).   "I do hope you'll have good sport, and find plenty of foxes."

Captain Forrard.   "Hope so.   By the way, how is that beautiful collie of yours that I admired so much?"

Mrs. Shodditon.   "Oh!   Fanny! poor dear! Our keeper shot it by mistake for a fox!"

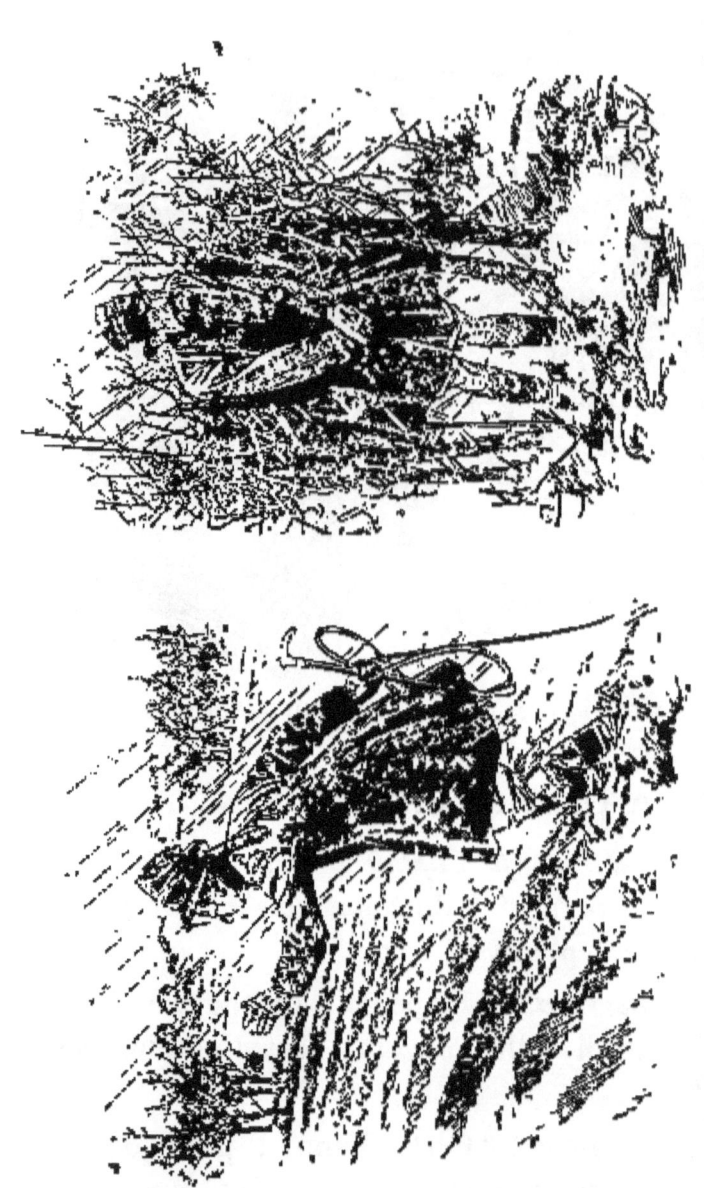

Short-sighted Party (thrown earlier, after weary tramp, thinks he sees mount on ploughed upland, and approaches busk coaxingly). "Whoa, my beauty! Steady, my gal, steady then," &c.

Same Short-sighted Party arrived at thornbush, discovers error and reflects—"Five miles from station, perhaps ten—fifty miles from town, missed express, missed dinner, lost mount, wet through, getting dusk, and, by the way, where am I?" *[Left reflecting.*

Gorgeous Stranger. "I say, Huntsman, would you mind blowing your horn two or three times? I want my fellow, who has my flask, to know where we are, don't you know!"

DIARY OF THE MODERN HUNT SECRETARY

["Capping all non-subscribers is pretty generally resorted to, this season, not only in the shires, but also with provincial packs."—*Daily Press.*]

Monday.—Splendid gallop after non-subscriber. Spotted the quarry on good-looking chestnut, whilst we were drawing big covert. Edged my horse over in his direction, but non-subscriber very wary—think he must have known my face as "collector of tolls." Retired again to far side of spinney and disguised myself in pair of false whiskers, which I always keep for these occasions. Craftily sidled up, and finally got within speaking distance, under cover of the whiskers, which effectually masked my battery. "Beg pardon, sir," I began, lifting my hat, "but I don't think I have the pleasure of knowing your name as a subscri——" But he was off like a shot. Went away over a nice line of country, all grass, and a good sound take-off to most of the fences. Non-subscriber had got away with about a three lengths lead of me, and that interval was fairly maintained for the first mile and a half of the race. Then,

Gent (who has just executed a double somersault and is somewhat dazed). "Now where the dickens has that horse gone to?"

ON EXMOOR

Gent (very excited after his first gallop with staghounds).
"Hi, mister, don't let the dogs maul 'im, and I'll take the
'aunch at a bob a pound!"

felt most annoyed to see that my quarry somewhat
gained on me as we left the pasture land and went
across a holding piece of plough. Over a stiff post
and rails, and on again, across some light fallow,

COOKED ACCOUNTS

Extract from old Fitzbadly's letter to a friend, describing a run in the Midlands :—"I was well forward at the brook, but lost my hat, and had to dismount."

towards a big dry ditch. The hunted one put his horse resolutely at it—must say he rode very straight, but what *won't* men do to avoid "parting?"—horse jumped short and disappeared from view together with his rider. Next moment I had also come a cropper at ditch, and rolled

"Hup —yer beast!"   "Hup!!—yer brute!"

down on top of my prey. "Excuse me," I said,
taking out my pocket-book and struggling to my
knees in six inches of mud, "but when you rather
abruptly started away from covertside, I was just
about to remark that I did not think you were a
subscriber, and that I should have much pleasure
in taking the customary 'cap'—thank you." And
he paid up quite meekly. We agreed, as we
rode back together, in the direction in which we
imagined hounds to be, that even if they had got
away with a good fox, the field would not be likely
to have had so smart a gallop as he and I had
already enjoyed. Lost my day's hunting, of course.

Thursday.—Got away after another non-sub-

scriber, and chased him over four fields, after which
he ran me out of sight.
Lost my day's hunting
again, but was highly
commended by
M.F.H. for my zeal.

Saturday.—M.F.H.
pointed out five non-
subscribers, and I at
once started off to
"cap" them. Lost
another day with
hounds—shall send in
my resignation.

" Hup ! ! !—yer infernal, confounded——Hover ! ! ! "

And " Hover " it was !

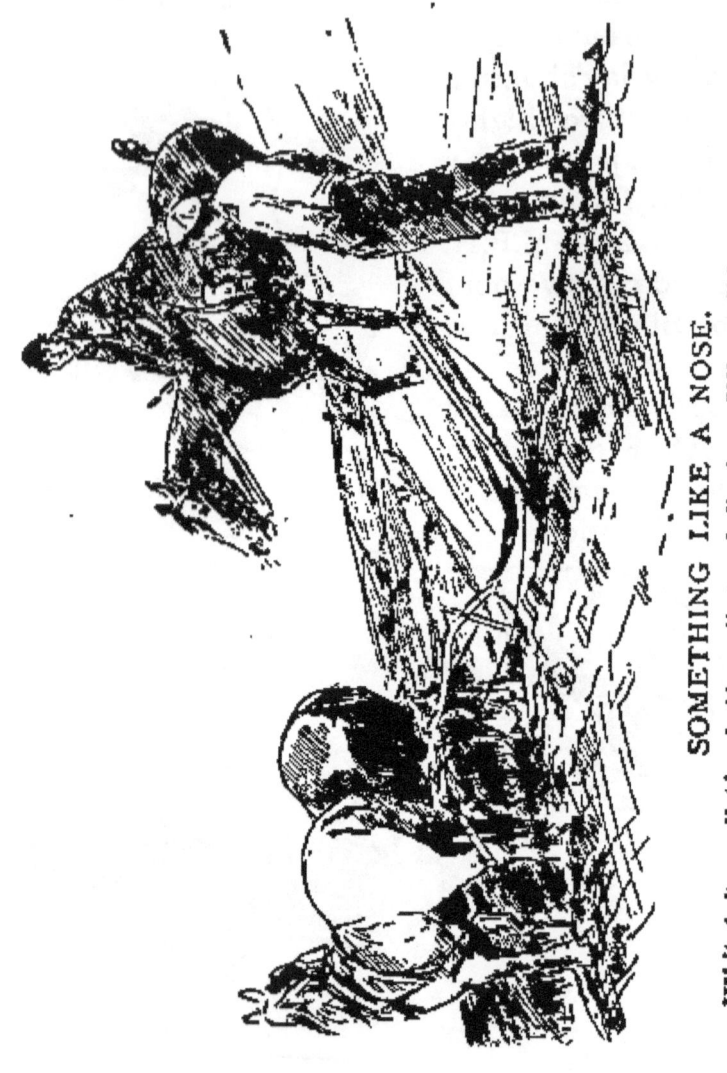

SOMETHING LIKE A NOSE.

Whip (after galloping half a mile to a hollow). "Where did you see him?"
Yokel. "Can't zay as 'ow I 'zactly zeed 'un, but I think I *smelled* 'un!"

Second Horseman No. 1. "Ulloah, Danny, what are you lookin' for?"

Second Horseman No. 2. "Perkisites. Guv'nor's just been over 'ere. 'E jumps so much 'igher than 'is 'orse, there's always some small change or summat to be picked up!"

THE NEW NIMROD.

[Mr. Pat O'Brien, M.P., was first in at the death on one occasion with the Meath Hounds on his bicycle, and was presented with the brush.]

AIR—"*The Hunting Day*"

" WHAT a fine hunting day "—
'Tis an old-fashioned lay
That I'll change to an up-to-date pome ;
 Old stagers may swear
 That the pace isn't fair,
But they're left far behind us at home !
See cyclists and bikes on their way,
And scorchers their prowess display ;
 Let us join the glad throng
 That goes wheeling along,
And we'll all go a-hunting to-day !

 New Nimrods exclaim,
 " Timber-topping " is tame,
And " bull-finches " simply child's play ;
 And they don't care a jot
 For a gallop or trot,
Though they *will* go a-hunting to-day.
There's a fox made of clockwork, they say.
They'll wind him and get him away ;
 He runs with a rush
 On rails with his brush,
So we must go and chase him to-day.

28

THE LANGUAGE OF SPORT.

"Where the——! What the——!! Who the——!!!
Why the——!!!!"

We've abolished the sounds
Of the horn and the hounds—
'Tis the bicycle squeaker that squeals
And the pack has been stuffed,
Or sent to old Cruft,
Now the huntsmen have taken to wheels!
Hairy country no more we essay,
Five bars, too, no longer dismay,
For we stick to the roads
In the latest of modes,
So we'll bike after Reynard to-day!

29

COMFORTING, VERY!

Sportsman (who has mounted friend on bolting mare) shouts. "You're all right, old chap! She's never been known to refuse water, and swims like a fish!"

Old Stubbles (having pounded the swells). " Aw—haw——! laugh away, but who be the roight side o' the fence, masters?"

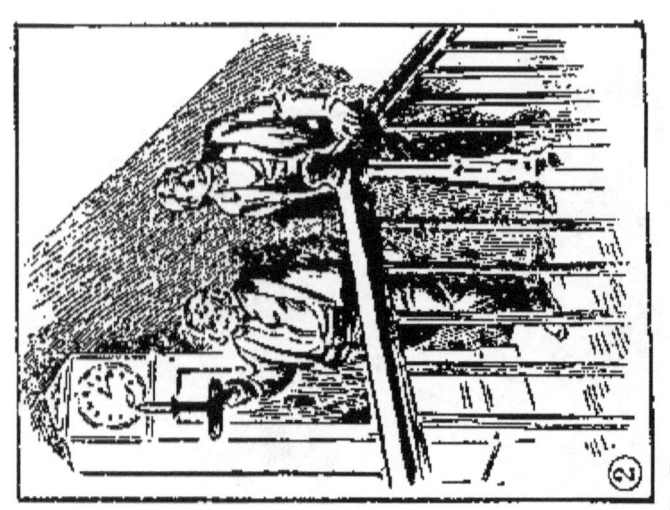

CUB HUNTING

1. "Ah, my boys," said Percy Johnson, "give me a good old hurry and scurry— Heigh O! gee whoa!—over the downs and through the brushwood after the cubs. So, early in the morning as you like. What can be more exhilarating?" 2. So, in happy anticipation of the morrow's meet, he retired.

3. Later, at 4 a.m., the butler came to rouse him. "Sir!" A pause. "Sir, th' 'osses be very nigh ready!" Uncertain voice from within—" Eh? good-night! Remember to call me early in the morning!" 4. Snoring resumed *in infinitum*. Still, Percy looked rather sheepish later on, when the others pretended they had missed him on the road, and inquired whether he had found the morning as exhilarating as he had expected.

MY LITTLE BROWN MARE

(A Song for the commencement of the Hunting Season)

SHE's rather too lean but her head's a large size,
And she hasn't the average number of eyes;
Her hind legs are not what you'd call a good pair,
And she's broken both knees, has my little brown mare.

You can find some amusement in counting each rib,
And she bites when she's hungry like mad at her crib;
When viewed from behind she seems all on the square,
She's quite a Freemason—my little brown mare.

Her paces are rather too fast, I suppose,
For she often comes down on her fine Roman nose,
And the way she takes fences makes hunting men stare.
For she backs through the gaps does my little brown mare.

She has curbs on her hocks and no hair on her knees;
She has splints and has spavins wherever you please?
Her neck, like a vulture's, is horribly bare,
But still she's a beauty, my little brown mare.

She owns an aversion to windmills and ricks,
When passing a waggon she lies down and kicks;
And the clothes of her groom she'll persistently tear—
But still she's no vice has my little brown mare.

When turned down to grass she oft strays out of bounds;
She always was famous for snapping at hounds;
And even the baby has learnt to beware
The too playful bite of my little brown mare.

34

TROUBLES OF A WOULD-BE SPORTSMAN

Huntsman (to W. B. S.). "Just 'op across, would ye, sir, and turn those 'ounds to me, please."

RESPICE FINEM

Excited Shepherd (to careful Sportsman, inspecting fence with slight drop). " Come on, sir! All right! Anywhere 'ere !"
Careful Sportsman. " All very fine! You want to give me a fall, and get half-a-crown for catching my horse !"

She prances like mad and she jumps like a flea,
And her waltz to a brass band is something to see :
No circus had ever a horse, I declare,
That could go through the hoops like my little brown mare.

I mount her but seldom—In fact, to be plain,
Like the Frenchman, when hunting I " do not remain :"
Since I've only one neck it would hardly be fair
To risk it in riding my little brown mare !

"WEEDS"

"'WARE WIRE!"

"Hallo, Jack! What's up?"   "Don' know! I'm not!"

MISPLACED ENERGY

Huntsman (seeking a beaten fox). " Now then, have you seen anything of him? "

Cockney Sportsman (immensely pleased with himself). " Well, rather! Why, I 've just driven him into this drain for you! "

"WHILE YOU WAIT"

"Here, my good man, just pull those rails down. Be as quick as you can!"

"Take 'em down, miss! It'll be a good four hours' job, for I've been all the mornin' a-puttin' of 'em up!"

ECHOES OF THE CHASE. BOXING DAY. "Where's the fox?"

Holiday Sportsman (to Whip, who has been hollering). "Gone away, of course."

Whip. "Gone away! Wotcher makin' all that noise for, then? I thought you'd caught 'im!"

EASILY SATISFIED

Gent (who all but dissolved partnership at the last fence). "Thank goodness I've got hold of the reins again! If I could but get my foot into that confounded stirrup, I should be all right!"

41

A NICE PROSPECT

Host (to Perks, an indifferent horseman, who has come down for the hunting). "Now, look here, Perks, old chap, as you're a light weight, I'll get you to ride this young mare of mine. You see, I want to get her qualified for our Hunt Cup, and she's not up to my weight, or I'd ride her myself. Perhaps I'd better tell you she hasn't been ridden to hounds before, so she's sure to be a bit nervous at first; and mind you steady her at the jumps, as she's apt to rush them; and I wouldn't take her too near other people, as she has a nasty temper, and knows how to use her heels; and, whatever you do, don't let her get you down, or she'll tear you to pieces. The last man that rode her is in hospital now. But keep your eye on her, and remember what I've said, and you'll be all right!"

[Consternation of Perks

'ARRY ON 'ORSEBACK

Our 'Arry goes 'unting and sings with a will,
"The 'orn of the 'unter is 'eard on the 'ill:"
And oft, when a saddle looks terribly bare,
The 'eels of our 'Arry are seen in the air!.

' W. STANDS FOR WIRE '

" Hulloah, Jarge! Been puttin' up some wire to keep the fox-hunter away?"

" Noa, I b'ain't put up no wire; but the 'unt they sends me a lot o' them boards with ' W' on um, so I just stuck 'em up all round the land, and they never comes nigh o' me now!"

THE HUNTING SEASON

Rector. "Is that the parcels post, James? He's early this morning, isn't he?" *(Noise without, baying of dogs, &c.)* "What's all this——"

James (excited). "Yes, sir. Postman says as how the young 'ounds, a comin' back from cubbin', found 'im near the kennels, and runned 'im all the way 'ere. They was close on 'im when he got in! Thinks it was a packet o' red 'errins in the bag, sir! I see the run from the pantry window"——*(with enthusiasm)*——"a beautiful ten minutes' bu'st, sir!"

" Duck, you fool! Duck !"

Hunting "Day by Day"

"The Mudsquashington Foxhounds had a good day's sport from Wotsisname Coverts (which were laid for a large number). They found in Thingamy Woods, rattled him round the Osier Beds, and then through the Gorse, just above Sumware. Leaving this and turning left-handed, he ran on as far as Sumotherplace, where he finally got to ground. Amongst the numerous field were Lord Foozle and Lady Frump, Messrs. Borkins, Poshbury, and Tomkyn-Smith." *

* Half a dozen similar paragraphs cut out as being too exciting for the average reader's brain to bear.—Ed.

At Melton

First Sportsman. "That crock of yours seems to be a bit of a songster."

Second Sportsman. "Yes, he has always been like that since I lent him to a well-known English tenor."

First Sportsman (drily). "You should have taken him in exchange."

A NICE BEGINNING.

The above is not a French bull-fight, but merely the unpleasant adventure Mr. Jopling experienced on our opening day, when a skittish Alderney crossed him at the first fence.

'ARRY ON 'ORSEBACK

'*Arry (in extremities).* "Well, gi' me a bike !"

CONVENIENCE OF A LIGHT-WEIGHT GROOM

Miss Ethel. "Now, sit tight this time, Charles. How could you be so stupid as to let him go?"

Voice from the ditch. "Don't jump here!"
Irish Huntsman. "And what would ye be after down there? Wather-cresses?"

RATHER

"Is fox-hunting dangerous?" asks one of our daily papers. A fox informs us that it has its risks.

Rough Rider (to old Creeper, who will not let his horse jump). "Now then, gov'nor, if you are quite sure you can't get under it, perhaps you'll let me 'ave a turn!"

PROOF POSITIVE

Podson (lately returned from abroad). "Well, I hear you've been having a capital season, Thruster."

Thruster. "Oh, rippin'! Why, I've had both collar-bones broken, left wrist sprained, and haven't got a sound horse left in my string!"

INEXPRESSIBLE

Master Jack (son of M.F.H., much upset by hard weather).
"Go skating with you! Not if I know it. May be all very
well for you women and those curate chaps—but we
hunting men, by George!!!"

BY THE COVERT SIDE

Fred (a notorious funk). "Bai Jove! Jack, I'm
afraid I've lost my nerve this season!"

Jack. "Have you? Doosid sorry for the poor
beggar who finds it!"

Elderly Sportsman. " I wonder they don't have that place stopped. Why, I remember running a fox to ground there twenty years ago ! Don't you ?"

THEORY AND PRACTICE; OR, WHY THE ENGAGEMENT WAS BROKEN OFF

Lady Di: (to Jack, whose vows of devotion have been interrupted by a fox being hollered away).
"Oh, Jack, my hair's coming down! Do stop and hold my horse. I won't be five minutes."

AWFUL RESULT OF THE WAR!

A Dream of Mr. Punch's Sporting Correspondent

["Mr. ARTHUR WILSON, Master of the Holderness Hunt, has received an intimation from the War Office that, in consequence of the war with the Transvaal, ten of his horses will be required."—*Daily Paper.*]

"NO FOLLOWERS ALLOWED"

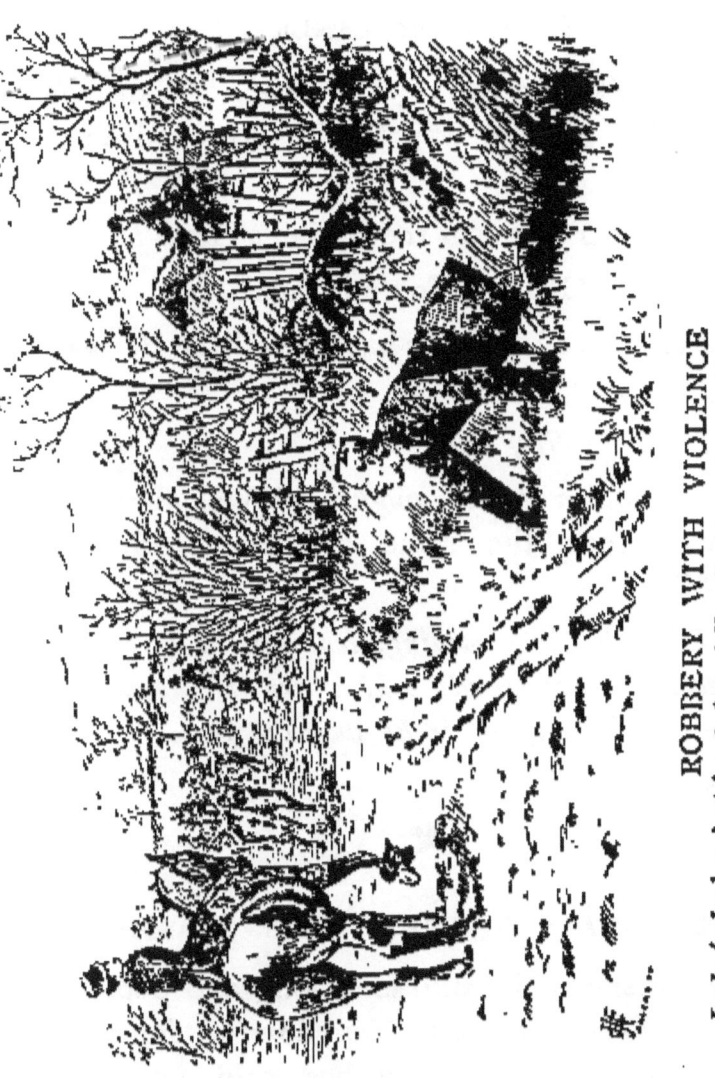

ROBBERY WITH VIOLENCE

Lady (who has just jumped on fallen Sportsman). "I'm awfully sorry! I hope we didn't hurt you?"

Fallen Sportsman. "Oh, I'm all right, thanks. But—er—do you mind leaving me my hat?"

In the Midlands

Belated Hunting Man (*to Native*). "Can you kindly point out the way to the Fox and Cock Inn?"

Native. "D'ye mean the Barber's Arms?"

B. H. M. "No, the Fox and Cock!"

Native. "Well, that's what we call the Barber's Arms."

B. H. M. "Why so?"

Native (*with a hoarse laugh*). "Well, ain't the Fox and Cock the same as the Brush and Comb?"

[*Vanishes into the gloaming, leaving the B. H. M. muttering those words which are not associated with benediction, while he wearily passes on his way.*

Appropriate to the Winter Season

For sportsmen, the old song long ago popular, entitled "*There's a Good Time Coming, Boys,*" if sung by a M.F.H. with a bad cold, as thus: "*There's a Good Tibe Cubbing, Boys!*"

Mr. Briggs's hunting cap comes home, but that is really a thing Mrs. Briggs *can* not, and *will* not put up with!

Mr. Briggs goes out with the Brighton Harriers. He
has a capital day. The only drawback is, that he is
obliged to lead his horse *up* hill to ease him—

and *down* hill because he is afraid of going over his head
—so that he doesn't get quite so much horse exercise as he
could wish!

AT THE HUNT BALL

(The Sad Complaint of a Man in Black)

O MOLLY, dear, my head, I fear, is going round and round,
Your cousin isn't in the hunt, when hunting men abound;
A waltz for me no more you'll keep, the girls appear to
think
There's a law been made in favour of the wearing of the
pink.
Sure I met you in the passage, and I took you by the hand,
And says I, " How many dances, Molly, darlint, will ye
stand ? "
But your card was full, you said it with a most owdacious
wink,
And I'm "hanging" all your partners for the wearing of
the pink!
You'd a waltz for Charlie Thruster, but you'd divil a
one for me,
Though he dances like a steam-engine, as all the world
may see;
'Tis an illigant divarsion to observe the crowd divide,
As he plunges down the ball-room, taking couples in his
stride.
'Tis a cropper you'll be coming, but you know your
business best,
Still, it's bad to see you romping round with Charlie and
the rest ;
Now you're dancing with Lord Arthur—sure, he's had
enough to dhrink—
And I'm "hanging" all your partners for the wearing of
the pink!
Your cruelty ashamed you'll be someday to call to mind,
You'll be glad to ask my pardon, then, for being so unkind,

MR. BRIGGS HAS ANOTHER DAY WITH THE HOUNDS

Mr. Briggs can't bear flying leaps, so he makes for a gap
—which is immediately filled by a frantic Protectionist,
who is vowing that he will pitchfork Mr. B. if he comes
" galloperravering " over his fences—danged if he doant !

The hunting men are first, to-night—well, let them have
 their whack—
You'll be glad to dance with me, someday—when all the
 coats are black !
But, since pink's the only colour now that fills your pretty
 head,
Bedad, I'll have some supper, and then vanish home to bed.
'Tis the most distressful ball-room I was ever in, I think,
And I'm "hanging " all your partners for the wearing of
 the pink !

A DOUBTFUL INFORMANT

Miss Connie (to Gent in brook). "Could you tell me if there is a bridge anywhere handy?"

NOT TO BE BEATEN

Cissy. "Why should they call the hare's tail the scut?"
Bobby (with a reputation as an authority to keep up). "Oh
—er—why you see—oh, of course, because the hare
scuttles, you know, when she is hunted."

WHY HE WAITED

"What's the matter with Jack's new horse?
He won't start."

"Don't know; but they say he's been in an
omnibus. Perhaps he's waiting for the bell!"

THE PLEASURES OF HUNTING

To get a toss in a snowdrift, and, while lying half-smothered, to be sworn at for not shouting to warn the man following you.

So Consoling

Lady (whose mare has just kicked a member of the Hunt, who was following too closely). "Oh, I'm so sorry! I do hope it didn't hurt you! She's such a gentle thing, and could only have done it in the merest play, you know."

POSITIVELY OSTENTATIOUS

Mr. Phunkstick (quite put out). "Talk about agricultural depression, indeed! Don't believe in it! Never saw fences kept in such disgustingly good order in my life!"

IRISH HUNTING TIPPLE

Englishman (having partaken of his friend's flask, feels as if he had swallowed melted lead). "Terribly strong! Pure whiskey, is it not?"

Irishman. "Faith! not at all! It's greatly diluted with gin!"

IN A SHOOTING COUNTRY

Railway Porter (who has been helping lady to mount). "I hope you'll 'ave a good day, ma'am."
Lady Diana. "I just hope we'll find a fox."
Porter (innocently). "Oh, that's all right, ma'am. The fox came down by the last train!"

INSULT TO INJURY

Fitz-Noodle's Harriers, after a capital run, have killed—a fox !

Incensed local M.F.H. "Confound it, sir, you have killed one of my foxes!"

F. N. "It's all right, old chap ! You may kill one of my hares !"

HUNTING SONG

*(To be sung when the Hounds meet at Colney Hatch
or Hanwell)*

TANTIVY! Anchovy! Tantara!
The moon is up, the moon is up,
  The larks begin to fly,
And like a scarlet buttercup
  Aurora gilds the sky.
Then let us all a-hunting go,
  Come, sound the gay French horn,
And chase the spiders to and fro,
  Amid the standing corn.
Tantivy! Anchovy! Tantara!

UNCOMMONLY KEEN

"Why, where's the horse, Miss Kitty? By
Jove, you're wet through! What has happened?"

"Oh, the stupid utterly refused to take that
brook, so I left him and swam it. I couldn't miss
the end of this beautiful thing!"

IN A BLIND DITCH

Sportsman (to friend, whom he has mounted on a raw four-year-old for "a quiet morning's outing"). "Bravo, Jack! Well done! That's just what the clumsy beggar wanted. Teach him to look where he's going!"

DRY HUMOUR

"Be'n't ye comin' over for 'im, mister?"

WIREPROOF

Sir Harry Hardman, mounted on " Behemoth," created rather a stir at the meet. He said he didn't care a hang for the barbed or any other kind of wire.

A SKETCH FROM THE MIDLANDS

"Hulloa, old chap! No! hurt, I hope?" "Oh, no, no! Just got off to have a look at the view."

74

Whip. "Here, here! Hold hard! Come back!"
Tommy (home for the holidays). "No jolly fear! You want to get first start!"

"BUSINESS FIRST"

Favourite Son of M.F.H. (to old huntsman). "No, Smith, you won't see much more of me for the rest of the season; if at all."

Smith (with some concern). "Indeed, sir! 'Ow's that?"

Son of M.F.H. "Well, you see, I'm reading hard."

Smith (interrogatively). "Readin' 'ard, sir?"

Son of M.F.H. "Yes, I'm reading Law."

Smith. "Well, I likes to read a bit o' them perlice reports myself, sir, now an' then; but I don't allow 'em to hinterfere with a honest day's 'untin'."

AN OMISSION BEST OMITTED

Brown (on foot). "Do you know what the total is for the season?"

Simkins (somewhat new to country life). "Fifteen pairs of foxes, the huntsman says. But he seems to have kept no count of rabbits or 'ares, and I know they've killed and eaten a lot of those!"

PUTTING IT NICELY

Young Lady (*politely, to old Gentleman who is fiddling with gap*). "I don't wish to hurry you, sir, but when you have quite finished your game of spillikins I should like to come!"

TERPSICHOREAN

Sportsman (to Dancing Man, who has accepted a mount).
" Hold on tight, sir, and she'll *waltz* over with you.

Benevolent Stranger. " Allow me, sir, to offer you a drink !"

Unfortunate Sportsman (just out of brook). " Thanks; but I've had a drop too much already !"

THE MAGIC WORD

Huntsman (having run a fox to ground, to yokel). " Run away down and get some o' your fellows to come up with spades, will ye?   Tell 'em we're after hidden treasure!"

A CAPITAL DODGE

Among his native banks Old Poddles takes a lot of
beating. He says there's nothing easier when you know
how to negotiate 'em.

HUNTING EXTRAORDINARY

JOBSON, who edits a cheerful little weekly, said to me the other day :

" You hunt, don't you ? "

I looked at him knowingly. Jobson interpreted my smile according to his preconceived idea.

" I thought so," he continued.

" Well, you might do me a bright little article— about half a column, you know—on hunting, will you ? "

Why should I hesitate ? Jobson is safe for cash ; and he had not asked me to give my own experiences of the hunting field. I replied warily, " I fancy I know the sort of thing you want."

"Good," he said, and before we could arrive at any detailed explanation he had banged the door and dashed downstairs, jumped into his hansom and was off.

This was the article :—

THOUGHTS ON HUNTING.

It is hardly possible to overrate the value of hunting as a National sport. Steeplechasing is a Grand-National sport, but it is the sport of the rich, whereas hunting is not. By judiciously

MANNERS IN THE FIELD

Always be prepared to give the lead to a lady, even at some little personal inconvenience.

dodging the Hunt Secretary, you can, in fact, hunt for nothing. Of course, people will come at me open-mouthed for this assertion, and say, "How about the keep of your horses?" To which I reply, "If you keep a carriage, hunt the carriage horse; if you don't, borrow a friend's horse for a long ride in the country, and accidentally meet the hounds." To proceed. This has been a season of poor scent. Of course, the horses of the present

THE PLEASURES OF HUNTING

Having been cannoned and nearly brought down, to be asked if you are trying the
American seat.

day have deteriorated as line hunters: they possess not the keen sense of smell which their grandsires had. But despite this the sport goes gaily on. There are plenty of foxes—but we cannot agree with the popular idea of feeding them on poultry. And yet, in every hunt, we see hunters subscribing to poultry funds. This is not as it should be: Spott's meat biscuit would be much better for foxes' food.

But these be details: let us hie forrard and listen to the cheery voice of sly Reynard as he is winded from his earth. The huntsman blows his horn, and soon the welkin rings with a chorus of brass instruments; the tufters dash into covert, and anon the cheerful note of *Ponto* or *Gripper* gives warning that a warrantable fox is on foot—well, of course, he couldn't be on horseback, but this is merely a venatorial *façon de parler*. Away go the huntsmen, showing marvellous dexterity in cracking their whips and blowing their horns at the same moment. Last of all come the hounds, trailing after their masters—ah, good dogs, you cannot hope to keep up very far with the swifter-footed horses! Nevertheless, they strain at their leashes and struggle for a better place at the horses' heels. "Hike forrard!

HUNTING SKETCH
The Cast Shoe, or Late for the Meat.

tally ho! whoo-hoop!" They swoop over the
fields like a charge of cavalry. But after several
hours' hard running a check is at hand: the fox
falters, then struggles on again, its tail waving over
its head. As its pursuers approach, it rushes up a
tree to sit on the topmost branch and crack nuts.

The panting horses arrive—some with their
riders still in the saddle, though many, alas! have
fallen by the wayside. Next come the hounds, at
a long interval—poor *Fido*, poor *Vic*, poor *Snap!*
you have done your best to keep up, but the horses

A KINDLY VIEW OF IT

First Rustic (to Second Ditto). "Oh, I say! Ain't he fond of his horse!"

have out-distanced you! The whipper-in immediately climbs the tree in which the little red-brown animal still peacefully cracks its nuts, its pretty tail curled well over its head. Its would-be captor carries a revolving wire cage, and, by sleight-of-hand movement, manages to get the quarry securely into it. Then he descends, places the cage in a cart and it is driven home.

The "mort" is sounded by four green velvet-coated huntsmen, with horns wound round their bodies; a beautiful brush presented to the lady who was first up at the "take"; and then the field slowly disperse. Tally Ho-Yoicks! all is over for the day.

M.F.H. "Hold hard! Hold hard, please!! Where *are* you going with that brute?"
Diana (plaintively). "I wish I knew!"

THE LAST DAY OF HUNTING

(Stanzas for the First of April)

RIGHT day to bid a long farewell
  To the field's gladsome glee;
To hang the crop upon its peg,
  The saddle on its tree.
All Fools' the day, all Fools' the deed,
  That hunting's end doth bring—
With all those stinking violets,
  And humbug of the Spring!

Good-bye to pig-skin and to pink,
  Good-bye to hound and horse!
The whimpering music sudden heard
  From cover-copse and gorse;
The feathering stems, the sweeping ears,
  The heads to scent laid low,
The find, the burst, the " Gone-away ! "
  The rattling " Tally-ho ! "

My horses may eat off their heads,
  My huntsman eat his heart;
My hounds may dream of kills and runs,
  In which they've borne their part,
Until the season's bore is done,
  And Parliament set free,
And cub-hunting comes back again
  To make a man of me !

89

"A-HUNTING WE WILL GO!"

Lady. "You're dropping your fish!"

Irish Fish Hawker (riding hard). "Och, bad luck to thim! Niver moind. Sure we're kapin' up wid the gentry!"

JUMPING POWDER

(*Mr. Twentystun having a nip on his way to covert*)

Small Boy. "Oh my, Billy, 'ere's a heighty-ton gun a chargin' of 'isself afore goin' into haction!"

DRAWN BLANK

Huntsman. "How is it you never have any foxes here now?"

Keeper (who has orders to shoot them). "Pheasants have eat 'em all!"

THE ADVANTAGE OF EDUCATION

M.F.H. (who has had occasion to reprimand hard-riding Stranger). "I'm afraid I used rather strong language to you just now."

Stranger. "Strong language? A mere *twitter*, sir. You should hear *our* Master!"

Irate Non-sporting Farmer. "Hi! you there! What the Duce do you mean by riding over my wheat!"

'Arry. "'Ere, I say! What are yer givin' us? *Wheat!* Why, it's only bloomin' mud!"

"Foot and Mouth" Trouble

A valuable hunter, belonging to Mr. Durlacher, got its hind foot securely fixed in its mouth one day last week, and a veterinary surgeon had to be summoned to its assistance. This recalls the ancient Irish legend of the man who never opened his mouth without putting his foot into it. But that, of course, was a bull.

Decidedly Not

Nervous Visitor (pulling up at stiff-looking fence). "Are you going to take this hedge, sir?"

Sportsman. "No. It can stop where it is, as far as I'm concerned.

Ungrateful

The Pride of the Hunt (to Smith, who, for the last ten minutes, has been gallantly struggling with obstinate gate). "Mr. Smith, if you really *can't* open that gate, perhaps you will kindly move out of the way, and allow me to *jump* it!"

APT

Brown (helping lady out of water). "'Pon my word, Miss Smith, you remind me exactly
of What's-her-name rising from the What-you-call!"

A CHECK

M.F.H. (*riding up to old Rustic, with the intention of asking him if he has seen the lost fox*). "How long have you been working here, master?"

Old Rustic (*not seeing the point*). "Nigh upon sixty year, mister!"

"WHAT'S IN A NAME?"

Whip. "Wisdom! Get away there!! Wisdom!! Wisdom!!! Ugh!—you always were the biggest fool in the back!"

SOMETHING THAT MIGHT HAVE BEEN
EXPRESSED DIFFERENTLY

Mrs. Brown (being helped out of a brook by the gallant Captain, who has also succeeded in catching her horse). "Oh' Captain Robinson! thank you *so* much !"

Gallant, but somewhat flurried, Captain. "Not at all— don't mention it." (*Wishing to add something excessively polite and appropriate.*) "Only hope I may soon have another opportunity of doing the same again for you."

REASSURING

Criticising friend (to nervous man on new horse). "Oh! now I recollect that mare. Smashem bought her of Crashem last season, and she broke a collar-bone for each of them."

"THE TIP OF THE MORNING TO YOU!"

First Whip thanks him, and hums to himself, "When other tips, and t'other parts, Then he remembers *me!*"

Giles (indicating Sportsman on excitable horse, waiting his turn). "Bless us all, Tumas, if that un beant a goin' to try it back'ards!"

WITH THE HARDUP HARRIERS

Dismounted Huntsman (to his mount). "Whoa, you old brute! To think I went and spared yer from the biler only last week! You hungrateful old 'idebound 'umbug!'"

(1) On Clothes.—" Why not employ local talent ? Saves half the money, and no one can tell the difference."

(2) If the thong of your whip gets under your horse's tail,
just try to pull it out!

(3) Don't buy a horse because he is described as being "Well known with the —— Hounds." It might be true.

(4) If at a meet your horse should get a bit out of hand, just run him up against some one.

(5) If opening a gate for the huntsman, don't fall into the middle of the pack!

(6) Sit well back at your fences!

(7) Look before you leap.

(8) If you lose your horse, just tell the huntsman to catch it for you.

EXCUSABLE

M.F.H. (*justly irate, having himself come carefully round edge of seed-field*). "Blank it all, Rogerson, what's the good o' me trying to keep the field off seeds, and a fellow like you coming slap across 'em?"

Hard-Riding Farmer. "It's all right. They're my own! Ar 've just come ower my neighbour's wheat, and ar couldn't for vary sham(e) miss my own sceads!"

ANXIOUS TO SELL

Dealer (*to Hunting Man, whose mount has* NOT *answered expectations*). "How much do you want for that nag o' yours, sir?"

Hunting Man. "Well, I'll take a hundred guineas."

Dealer. "Make it *shillings*."

H. M. (*delighted*). "He's yours!"

NOT A LADIES' DAY

Miss Scramble. " Now, Charles, give me one more long hair-pin, and I shall do."

CASUAL

Owner of let-out hunters (to customer just returned from day's sport). "Are you aware, sir, that ain't my 'orse?"

Sportsman. "Not yours! Then, by Jove, I *did* collar the wrong gee during that scrimmage at the brook!"

AT OUR OPENING MEET

Stranger from over the water. "I guess you've a mighty smart bunch of dogs there, m'lord!"

Noble but crusty M.F.H. "Then you guess wrong, sir. *This is a pack of hounds!*"

MUST BE HUNGRY

"Wish you'd feed your horse before he comes out."

"Eh—why—hang it!—what do you mean?"

"He's always trying to eat my boots. He evidently thinks there's some chance of getting at a little corn!"

THE RETORT COURTEOUS

(A Reminiscence of the past Harrier Season)

Major Topknot, M.H. (to butcher's boy). "Hi! Hulloah! Have you seen my hare?"

Butcher's Boy. "Ga-a-rn! 'Ave you seen my whiskers?"

DISINTERESTED KINDNESS

Sportsman (just come to grief, to Kindhearted Stranger who has captured horse). "I say, I'm awfully obliged to you! I can get on all right, so please don't wait!"

Kindhearted Stranger. "Oh, I'd rather, thanks! I want you to flatten the next fence for me!"

ENCOURAGING

Nervous Man (who hires his hunters). "Know anything about this mare? Ringbone tells me she's as clever as a man!"

Friend. "Clever as a man? Clever as a woman more like it! Seen her play some fine old games with two or three fellows, I can tell you!"

NUNC AUT NUNQUAM

Voice from bottom of ditch. "Hold hard a minute! My money has slipped out of my pockets, and it's all down here somewhere!"

H 2

A REFORMED CHARACTER

John. "Goin' to give up 'untin'! Deary! deary! An' 'ow's that, missie ? "

Little Miss Di. " Well, you see, John, I find my cousin Charlie, who is going to be a curate, does not approve of hunting women, so I intend to be a district visitor instead ! "

MOTTOES; OR, "WHO'S WHO?"

Mrs. Prettyphat.　Family Motto—"*Medici jussu.*"

Something like a Character

Huntsman (on being introduced to future wife of M.F.H.). " Proud to make your acquaintance, miss! Known the Capting, miss, for nigh on ten seasons, and never saw 'im turn 'is 'ead from hanything as was jumpable! Knows a 'oss and knows a 'ound! Can ride one and 'unt t'other; and if that ain't as much as can be looked for in a 'usband, miss, why, I'll be jiggered!"

A Liberal Allowance

Huntsman (who has just drawn Mr. Van Wyck's coverts blank). " Rather short of cubs, I'm afraid, sir!"

Mr. Van Wyck (who has very recently acquired his country seat). " Most extraordinary! Can't understand it at all! Why, I told my keeper to order a dozen only last week!"

STORIES WITHOUT WORDS

How "the second horseman" went home.

Scene—*As above.*   Time—*Mid-day.*   Sport—*None up to now.*

Stout Party (about to leave). "Most extr'ordinary thing. Whenever I go home, they always have a rattling good run."

Candid Friend. "Then, for goodness' sake, *go home at once!*"

MOST EXTRAORDINARY

Dismounted Sportsman. "Now, how the deuce did my hat manage to get up there?"

STRAIGHT

Huntsman (*to Boy, who is riding his second horse*). "Hi, there! What the doose are yer doin' of with that second 'oss?"

Boy (*Irish, and only just come to the Hunt stables from a Racing Establishment*). "Arrah thin, if oi roides oi roides to win! and divil a second is he goin' to be at all, at all!!"

FORBEARANCE

Member of Hunt (*to Farmer*). "I wouldn't ride over those seeds if I were you. They belong to a disagreeable sort of fellow, who might make a fuss about it."

Farmer. "Well, sir, as him's me, he won't say nothing about it to-day."

*(Extract from a letter received by Mr. Shootall on the morning
when hounds were expected to draw his covers)*

Leadenhall Market, Thursday.

Sir,—Your esteemed order to hand. We regret that we
are quite out of foxes at present; but, as you mentioned
they were for children's pets, we thought guinea pigs might
do instead, so are sending half a dozen to-day. Hoping,
&c., &c.

Too Much

(Pity the Sorrows of a poor Hunting Man!)

Sportsman (suffering from intense aberration of mind in consequence of the weather, in reply to wife of his bosom). "Put out? Why, o' course I'm put out. Been just through the village, and hang me if at least half a dozen fools haven't told me that it's nice seasonable weather!"

At the Hunt Ball

Mr. Hardhit. "Don't you think, Miss Highflier, that men look much better in pink—less like waiters?"

Miss Highflier. "Yes, but more like ringmasters—eh?"

[*Hardhit isn't a bit offended, but seizes the opportunity.*

HINTS TO BEGINNERS

In mounting your horse, always stand facing his tail.

The patent pneumatic tennis-ball hunting costume. Falling a pleasure.

Second Whip. "G-aw-ne away!"

Middle-aged Diana. "Go on away, indeed! Impertinence! I'll go just when I'm ready!"

A CASE OF REAL DISTRESS

Fox-hunter. " Here's a bore, Jack ! The ground is half a
foot thick with snow, and it's freezing like mad ! "

THE HUNTSMAN'S POINT OF VIEW.

One of the best runs of the season.

Good scent all the way.

Sir Heavistone Stogdon unfortunately fell at a
stiff bank and broke his collar-bone.

At the last moment, I regret to say, the fox got
away.

A FOX HUNT

(After a tapestry)

BUGGLES WITH THE DEVON AND SOMERSET

He encounters a "coomb," and wonders if it is soft at the bottom.

WITH THE DEVON AND SOMERSET

Sportsman (from the bog). "Confound you, didn't you say there was a sound bottom here?"

Shepherd. "Zo there be, maister; but thou 'aven't got down to un yet!"

BUGGLES WITH THE DEVON AND SOMERSET

How he found a " Warrantable Deer."

BUGGLES WITH THE DEVON AND SOMERSET

In Devonshire.

133

FOOLS AND THEIR MONEY—

Jones (who has been having a fair bucketing for the last half-hour, as he passes friend, in his mad career). "I'd give a fiver to get off this brute!"

Friend (brutally). "Don't chuck your money away, old chap! You'll be off for less than that!"

WITH THE QUEEN'S

Leading Sportsman. "Hold ha—rd! Here's some more of that confounded barbed wire! Dashed if I don't think this country is mainly inhabited by retired fishing-tackle makers!"

[*Makes for nearest gate, followed by sympathetic field.*

HIS OPINION

Jenkinson (to M.F.H., who dislikes being bothered). "What do you think of this horse?" (*No answer.*) "Bred him myself, you know!"

M.F.H. (looking at horse out of corner of his eye). "Umph! I thought you couldn't have been such a silly idiot as to have *bought* him!"

THE VOICE OF SPRING

Bibulous Binks. "Gad, it's freezing again!"

A BLANK—BLANK—DAY

WHOSE FAULT?

"He *can* jump, but he *won't* !"

A VIEW HALLOO

(Hounds at fault)

Whip (bustling up to young Hodge, who has just begun to wave his cap and sing out lustily). " Now then, where is he ? "

Young H. " Yonder, sir ! Acomin' across yonder ! "

Whip. " Get out, why there ain't no fox there, stoopid ! "

Young H. " No, sir; but there be our Billy on I' jackass ! "

Miss Nelly (to her Slave, in the middle of the best thing of the Season). "Oh, Mr. Rowel, do you mind going back ? I dropped my whip at the last fence !"

SEVERE

M.F.H. (to Youth from neighbouring Hunt, who has been making himself very objectionable). " Now, look here, young man. I go cub-hunting for the purpose of educating *my own* puppies. As you belong to another pack, I 'll thank you to take yourself home ! "

HUNTING MEMORANDUM

Appearance of things in general to a gentleman who has just turned a
complete somersault ! !

* &c., &c., represent sparks of divers beautiful colours.

"LE SPORTMAN"

"Hi! Hi! Stop ze chasse! I tomble—I faloff! Stop ze fox!"

"CUBBING EVENTS CAST THEIR SHADOWS"

Half-awakened un-enthusiastic Sportsman (who wished to go out cub-hunting, but has entirely changed his mind, drowsily addressing rather astonished burglar). "Awright, old boy. Can't come with you this morning. Too sleepy."

[*Turns round and resumes deep sleep where he left off.*]

A BROKEN PLEDGE

Sportsman on bank (to Friend in brook). "Hallo, Thompson, is that you? Why, I thought you had joined the 'No Drinks in between Meals' Party!"

"In the Dim and Distant Future"

First Sportsman (cantering along easily). " I say, we shall see you at dinner on the nineteenth, shan't we ? "

Second Ditto (whose horse is very fresh, and bolting with him). " If the beast goes on like this—hanged if you'll ever see me again."

THERE'S LIFE IN THE OLD DOG YET

Ex-M.F.H. (eighty-nine and paralytic). "Fora-a-d ! Fora-a-d ! Fora-a-d ! "

Huntsman (making a cast for the line of the fox, near a railway). "Hold hard, please! Don't ride over the line!"

Would-be Thrusters. "Oh, no, we won't. There's a bridge farther on!"

"RANK BLASPHEMY"

Squire Oldboy, M.H. (*enjoying a long and very slow hunt*). "There she goes!
Afraid it's a new bare though."
Bored Sportsman. "How lucky! The other must be getting doosid old."

A CHECK

Huntsman. "Seen the fox, my boy?" *Boy.* "No, I ain't!"

Huntsman. "Then, what are you hollarin' for?"

Boy (who has been scaring rooks) "Cos I'm paid for it!"

EASIER SAID THAN DONE

Sixteen-stone Sportsman (who has been nearly put down from a "rotten" landing, to little Bricks, 9st. 2lb.): "Do you mind putting me back in the saddle, sir?".

THE TROUBLES OF AN M.F.H.

M.F.H. (to stranger, who is violently gesticulating to hounds). "When you have done *feeding your chickens,* sir, perhaps you will allow me to hunt my hounds!"

Nobody was near hounds in the big wood when
they pulled down the cub except Mr. Tinkler and his
inamorata. He rashly volunteers to secure the brush
for her!

" Morning, Tom. What a beastly day ! "
" It ain't a day, sir. I call it an interval between two
bloomin' nights ! "

A BAD LOOK-OUT

Sportsman (to Friend whom he has mounted). "For goodness' sake, old chap, don't let her put you down! She's certain to savage you!"

ECHOES OF THE CHASE

Huntsman (who has been having a very bad ride). " Either master wants some new 'orses or a new 'untsman !"

HINTS ON HUNTING

Always see that your bridle reins are sound. There are times when they have a considerable strain on 'em!

SO FAR, NO FARTHER

Extraordinary position assumed by Mr. Snoodle on the sudden and unexpected refusal of his horse.

HARD LUCK

Small Child (to Mr. Sparkin, who had come out at an unusually early hour in order to meet his inamorata at the guide-post, and pilot her out cub-hunting). "I was to tell you she has such a bad cold she couldn't come. But I'm going with you instead, if you promise to take care of me. I'm her cousin, you know!"

A PSEUDO-THRUSTER

Farmer (to Sportsman, returning from the chase) "Beg pardon, sir, but ain't you the gent that broke down that there gate of mine this morning?"

Mr. Noodel (who never by any chance jumps anything—frightfully pleased). "Er—did I? Well, how much is the damage?"

THE WATER TEST

Whip (bringing on tail hounds, in the rear of the field). "Hulloah! Who've you got there?"

Runner (who has just assisted sportsman out of a muddy ditch). "Dunno. Can't tell till we've washed 'im down a bit!"

MOST UNFORTUNATE

Horrible catastrophe which happened to Captain Fussey (our ladies' man) on his arrival at the opening meet. New coat, new boots, new horse, new everything! Hard luck!

A SEVERE TEST

Miss Sally (who has just taken off her mackintosh—to ardent admirer). " Look ! they're away ! Do just stuff this thing into your pocket. I'm sure I shan't want it again ! "

A STUDY IN EXPRESSION

Irate M.F.H. (who has had half an hour in the big gorse trying to get a faint-hearted fox away, galloping to "holloa" on the far side of covert). "Confound you and your pony, sir! Get out of my way!"

> [*Little Binks, who has been trying to keep out of people's way all day, thinks he can quite understand the feelings of the hunted fox.*

OUR HUNT "POINT TO POINT"

LAST week our Point to Point steeplechase came off. So did several of the riders : this merely *par parenthèse*. I offered to mark out the course, and, as I intended to escape the dread ordeal of riding by scratching my horse at the last moment, I thought it would be great fun to choose a very stiff, not to say bloodthirsty, line. Awful grumbling on the part of those unhappy ones who were to ride. Just as the bell rang for saddling, Captain Sproozer, ready dressed for the fray, came up to me with very long face, and said, "Beastly line this, you know, Phunker. I call it much too stiff."

I smiled in pitying and superior manner. "Think so, my dear Sproozer? My horse can't run, worse luck, but I only wish *I* were going to have the gallop over it."

"So you shall, then !" cried a rasping voice, suddenly, from behind me. Sir Hercules

AMENITIES OF SPORT

Huntsman (to Whip, sent forward for a view). "Haven't ye seen him, Tom?"
Whip. "No, sir."
Huntsman. "If he'd been in a pint pot, ye jolly soon would!"

HIS LITTLE DODGE

*First Hunting Man (having observed the ticket with " K "
on it in his friend's hat).* " I didn't know that old gee of
yours was a kicker. He looks quiet enough."

Second Hunting Man. " Well, he isn't really. I only
wear the " K " to make people give me more room ! "

Blizzard was the speaker, an awful man with an awful temper. "So you shall. My idiot of a jockey broke his collar-bone trying to jump one of the fences on this confounded course of yours to-day, so, as I am without a rider, you shall ride my mare Dinah."

Swallowed lump in my throat as I thanked him for his offer, but thought I had better decline, as I didn't know the mare, and besides that, I——

"Oh! all right, I know what you are going to say : that you're not much good on a horse "— (nothing of the sort!   I was not going to say any such thing, confound the man!)   "Of course, I know all that, and that you're not much of a rider ; but I can't help myself now. It's too late to get a decent horseman, so I shall have to make shift with you."

Deuced condescending of him. I made a feeble effort to escape, and would cheerfully have paid a hundred pounds for the chance of doing so. Phil Poundaway, great friend of mine, came up and said (sympathetically, as I thought at first), "I should think you'd prefer to get off it, wouldn't you, Phunker ? "

TRUE COURAGE

Whip. "Hi, sir! Keep back! The fox may break covert there!"

Foreigner. "Bah! I fear him not—your fox."

THE FORCE OF HABIT

Spanner (a great cyclist, whose horse has been startled by man on covert hack). "Hi! confound you! Why the deuce don't you sound your bell!!"

Thought he would volunteer in my place, so was perfectly frank with him. "My dear Phil, I'd give a hundred to get off——"

"Ah! you will, I expect, at the first fence, without paying the money!" he grinned, as he turned away.

Murder was in my heart at that moment. I got on Dinah, and, feeling like death, rode down to the starting-post. Thoughts of a misspent youth, of home and friends and things, came o'er me. I seemed once more to see the little rose-covered porch, the——

"What on earth are you mooning about?" thundered the Blizzardian voice in my ear. "Take hold of her head tighter than that, or you'll be off!"

The next moment the starter yelled "Go!" and away, like a whirlwind, we sped across the first field, towards a huge, thick blackthorn fence, the one I had thought to see such fun with. Fun! I never felt less funny in my life, as we approached it at the rate of two thousand miles an hour! The mare jumped high, but I jumped much higher, and seemed for a brief moment to be soaring through

"THE CART WITHOUT THE HORSE"

Scene—*Cub-hunting.*   Time—*About one o'clock.*

Lady. "Well, Count, what have you lost? Your lunch?"

The Count (who breakfasted some time before six o'clock, a.m.). "No, no! Donner und wetter! I have him, but I have lost my teeth!"

HORRIBLE PREDICAMENT

Gent (on mettlesome hireling). "'Elp! 'Elp! Somebody stop 'im! 'E's going to jump, and I can't!"

MOST EMBARRASSING

Lady (hiding behind bush, to Mr. Spoodle, who has captured her horse). "Oh, thank you so much! But I hope to goodness you have found my skirt as well!"

[*Nice position for Mr. Spoodle, who is very bashful, and has seen nothing of the garment.*

"DO NOT SPEAK TO THE MAN AT THE WHEEL"

'Arry (puffing a "twopenny smoke," to huntsman, making unsuccessful cast). "Very bad scent."

Huntsman. "Shockin'! Smells like burnin' seaweed!"

OBEYING ORDERS

"It's all very well for master to say 'Keep close to Miss Vera, Miles'—but I want to know 'oo's going to take Miles to the 'orsepital?"

GALLANTRY REWARDED

Lady (having had a fall at a brook, and come out the wrong side,—to stranger who has caught her horse). "Oh, I'm so much obliged to you! Now, do you mind just bringing him over?"

JUST OFF

" Ride her on the snaffle, Tom !   Don't ride her on the curb !"
" Hang your curb and snaffle !   I've enough to do to *ride her on the saddle !* "

A Suggestion : No more trouble from wire, damage to fences, etc.

the blue empyrean. Somehow, the mare managed to evade me on the return journey earthwards, and, instead of alighting on the saddle, I found myself "sitting on the floor." A howl—it might have been of sympathy, but it didn't sound quite like that—arose from the crowd, and then I thought that I would go home on foot, instead of returning to explain matters to Sir Hercules. As a matter of fact, I don't much care for associating with old Blizzard, at all events, not just now.

THE TRIALS OF AN M.F.H.

M.F.H. (to misguided enthusiast who has been cheering hounds on a bad scent). "Now then! Am I going to hunt the hounds or are you?" *Enthusiast (sweetly).* "Just as you please, m'lord, just as you please."

OFF HIS GUARD

Farmer (just coming up). "Young gentleman riding your brown horse, my lord, had nasty accident a field or two back. Barbed wire—very ugly cuts!"

My Lord. "Tut—tut—tut! Dear—dear—dear! Not the horse, I hope?"

"BON VOYAGE!"

Mossu (shot into a nice soft loam), exultingly. "A—ha—a! I am safe o·vère! Now it is your turn, Meester Timbre Jompre! Come on, sare!"

M 2

THE OTHER SIDE OF THE BRIDGE

ON THE WAY HOME FROM THE EXMOOR HUNT—NO KILL

Fair Huntress. "What a pity the hounds let that splendid stag get away, Colonel, wasn't it?"

Colonel. "Pity! Ha, if they'd only taken my advice we should have been up with him now, instead of being miles away on the wrong track!"

Distinguished Foreigner (to good Samaritan who has caught his horse). "Merci bien, monsieur! You save me much trouble. Before, I lose my horse—I lose him altogether, and I must put him in the newspaper!"

VIVE LA CHASSE!

Foreign Visitor (an enthusiastic "sportsman," viewing fox attempting to break). "A-h-h-h! Halte-la! Halte! You shall not escape!"

RATHER TOO MUCH

Lady (having just cannoned Stranger into brook). "Oh, I'm *so* sorry I bumped you! Would you mind going in again for my hat?"

THE END OF THE HUNTING SEASON

(By Our Own Novice)

GOOD-BYE to the season !   E'en gluttons
　Have had quite enough of the game,
And if we returned to our muttons,
　Our horses are laid up and lame.
We hunted straight on through the winter,
　And never were stopped by the frost,
As I know right well from each splinter
　Of bone that my poor limbs have lost.

Good-bye to the season !   The " croppers"
　I got where the fences were tall,
And Oh the immaculate "toppers"
　That always were crushed by my fall.
Don't think though that I'm so stout-hearted
　As e'er to jump hedges or dikes,
It's simply that after we've started,
　My " gee " gallivants as it likes.

In vain I put on natty breeches,
　And tops like Meltonian swell,
It ends in the blessed old ditches,
　I know like the Clubs in Pall Mall.

184

HINTS TO BEGINNERS
Good hands will often make the most confirmed refuser
jump.

TRULY DELIGHTFUL!

Galloping down the side of a field covered with mole-hills, on a
weak-necked horse, with a snaffle bridle, one foot out of your stirrup, and
a bit of mud in your eye!

SELF-PRESERVATION

Tomlin (who has been mounted by friend). "It's all very well to shout 'Loose your reins,' but what the deuce *am* I to hang on to?"

And when from a " gee " that's unruly
　　I fall with a terrible jar,
I know that old *Jorrocks* spoke truly,
　　And hunting's " the image of war."

And never for me "*Fair Diana* "
　　Shall smile as we know that she can,
With looks that are sweeter than manna,
　　On many a fortunate man.
It adds to the pangs that I suffer,
　　When thrown at a fence in her track,
To hear her " Ridiculous duffer ! "
　　When jumping slap over my back.

I've fractured my ulnar, I'm aching
　　Where over my ribs my horse rolled ;
Egad ! the " Old Berkeley " is making
　　One man feel uncommonly old.
Good-bye to the season !　I 'm shattered
　　And damaged in figure and face ;
But thankful to find I'm not scattered
　　In pieces all over the place !

SEASONABLE DISH FOR A SPORTSMAN.—A plate
*o' f*ox-tail soup.

THE RULE OF THE HUNTING-FIELD.—Lex
Tally-ho-nis.

FASHIONABLE FOOD FOR HORSES.—Hay *à la*
mowed.

QUOTATIONS GONE WRONG
"Life has passed
With me but roughly since I heard thee last."
Cowper.

ALL HER PLAY

Country Gentleman (to nervous man, whom he has mounted). "By Jove, old chap, never saw the mare so fresh! Take care you ain't off!" *Nervous Man (heartily).* "W——wish to goodness I were!"

HINTS TO BEGINNERS

Always let your horse see that you are his master.

THE END

BRADBURY, AGNEW, & CO. LD., PRINTERS, LONDON AND TONBRIDGE.